The Sorcerer's Apprentice

by

Robin Muller

Kids Can Press

NCE upon a time, an orphan named Robin packed his belongings and set out to look for work. The fellow had no trade, but he was clever and brave and, what was more, he could read and write.

He stopped at every village and town along the way, but no one had work for him.

Late one night, tired and hungry, Robin came to the edge of a forest. Through the trees he could see the flicker of yellow light.

"Perhaps it is a fire in a cottage hearth," he thought. "No doubt a big pot of stew is simmering." He decided to find the house and ask for food and shelter for the night.

In the darkened woods, owls darted before him, and branches stretched out as if to bar his way. Unafraid, he hurried toward the light. But instead of a cozy cottage, there loomed before him a ruined old house, dark and crumbling.

Robin bravely knocked on the door. With a thundering crack, the door opened and a tall man, with eyes like ice, peered down at him.

"Why have you disturbed me?" he demanded.

"Please, sir," said the lad, "I mean no harm. I am a poor orphan looking for work. I hoped you might give me some food and shelter for the night."

The strange man thought for a moment. "I could use an apprentice," he growled. "Tell me, can you read and write?"

"Yes, sir," Robin replied proudly.

"Then," snarled the man, "you are no use to me," and he began to close the door.

But the clever lad thought quickly. "Read and write," he bellowed, "I thought you said eat and fight. Those I can do very well, but reading and writing are two things I know nothing about."

"If this is true," replied the man, "you will suit me." He eyed the lad suspiciously as he opened the door wide.

By the dim light, Robin surveyed his new home. Everything was old and ugly—everything except a golden cage which hung from a rafter and held a beautiful white dove.

"Your duties," began the man, "will be to cook my meals, stoke the fire, prepare ingredients for my experiments and," he added, pointing at the dove, "tend my little pet. But if I find you have been lazy or meddled in matters that don't concern you, you will regret it."

He told the lad to make himself a bed of straw in a corner, then he brought him a loaf of stale bread and some cold, thin soup.

"Eat quickly," he said, "then sleep, for in the morning, you shall work harder than you ever have before."

After his meal, Robin lay on his bed and wondered why his new master would prefer a fool for a helper.

"There is something strange about this," he murmured. "I had best keep my eyes and ears open."

Days passed, and the apprentice slaved from dawn to dusk. At night he would lie on his rough bed and listen to the dove cooing, like a soft, sweet lullaby.

The apprentice soon grew to love the little bird. It hurt him to see the dove caged and at the mercy of their master, for the man tormented it cruelly, swearing terrible oaths should the dove ever try to escape.

One morning the man announced he was going on a short journey.

"I shall return before dusk," he said. "Keep to your chores and don't touch anything you shouldn't. If I find you have disobeyed me, you will regret you were ever born." Without saying goodbye, he disappeared among the trees.

Although Robin pretended to be stupid, he had watched his master carefully and realized that the man was an evil sorcerer.

"Sorcery—now that is an art I would love to master," he said aloud, "for with a book of charms, I might do some good in the world."

"May I help?" asked a small voice.

The apprentice jumped to his feet and looked around.

"May I help?" the voice asked again.

This time Robin knew who had spoken. It was the dove.

"How can you help me?" he asked. "What I need to know can only come from the study of a book of magic. And even then," he said with a shudder, "I fear what my master would do if he discovered I could read."

"In his private chamber," answered the dove, "the sorcerer keeps his books of wizardry. If you free me, I will keep watch while you are studying and warn you when he returns."

The apprentice thought for a moment, considering the risk. But his desire to learn overcame his fear, and he freed the little bird. The dove flew out the window and sailed high over the trees.

Robin crept up the tower's twisting stair. At the top, a huge door rose before him. He pushed with all his strength, and the door swung open.

Every corner of the room was filled with books—from huge volumes tattered with age, to the tiniest diaries wrapped in silk. As Robin looked around in awe, a large, black book lying alone on a table, fastened with a lock of iron, seemed to beckon him. The lad shivered with fear. Quickly he chose another volume, blew the dust from its cover, and opened it. A comet's tail burst from the page, showering the room with a shimmering cascade of rainbow-coloured stars.

Robin read page after page of great spells and small spells until, like a pool that clears as you look into its depths, he could see all that moved on earth and beyond into the heavens.

An urgent flutter of wings roused him from his studies.

"Hurry," cried the dove, "the sorcerer is coming through the clearing. You must hurry or he will catch you."

Returning the book to its place, Robin rushed from the room.

But he cried out when he saw that he had forgotten his chores.

"I am lost," he said, remembering the sorcerer's terrible warning.

"Don't despair," cooed the dove. "While in the cage I'm helpless, but free, I have my own power." And she began flying around the room.

Suddenly everything sprang to life. Crockery danced through the air and came to rest clean and wiped, the kindling chopped and stacked itself neatly, and the fire began to blaze.

When the sorcerer entered, the room was perfectly tidy, and the lad was standing by the table, the supper ready and hot.

Soon Robin began to notice a change in his master. Where before the man had been stern with him and taunting to the dove, now he seemed almost light-hearted.

One grey morning the sorcerer called the apprentice.

"The King, my brother, has died, leaving no heir. I shall take his place," he gloated, "and you will inform the people of my intention. Go, and return when you know how they intend to receive me."

When the apprentice reached the palace, he was ushered into the great hall where the wise men had gathered. They listened to the sorcerer's offer in silence. When the apprentice finished, the court broke into a flurry of whispers.

An old man dressed in robes of velvet and gold stepped forward.

"This is a sorrowful land now that we have lost our King," he said, "for he was a kind-hearted ruler and all his people loved him.

"But he was not the last of his line as you suggest. The King has an heir, a lovely little girl who, from the moment of her birth, filled the palace with joy.

"One stormy night she mysteriously disappeared. A small white feather on her pillow and the paw print of a wolf were all that we ever found. I fear," he said sadly, "that it was from broken hearts that first the Queen and then the King died, believing they would never see their dear child again.

"Some believe that one day she will return," he sighed. "But even without this hope, we would not have your master as our ruler. He is a worker of evil who, many times, has sent his wickedness to trouble our land."

When the apprentice returned with the councillors' decision, the sorcerer flew into a rage.

"Not have me as their King," he roared, "they shall regret their foolishness. I will send dragons to scorch their land and eat their cattle; or perhaps, a host of howling witches to fly above their beds at night and drive them all mad." The sorcerer ran up the tower stairs.

The apprentice, frightened by the man and exhausted from his journey, fell into a troubled sleep.

Next morning Robin woke with a start to find his master's face peering into his own.

"Get up," he cried, "we must begin without delay. I have chosen the punishment for those fools, but the spell will take time. This will be my triumph, the greatest act of wickedness the world has ever known! And," he added, glaring at the lad, "you shall assist me."

Reluctantly the apprentice did everything the sorcerer demanded, until, finding a moment alone, he approached the golden cage.

"Little dove," he whispered, "how can we stop the sorcerer?"

"Only by his own devices," replied the dove. "Tonight while he sleeps, you must visit his chamber and study his books. In them you may find a way to defeat him."

So that night, while his master snored, Robin lit a candle and, silent as a shadow, climbed the stairs.

The sorcerer's room was as he had remembered. But now, in the flickering candlelight, the black, iron-bound book seemed more dreadful than before.

All night Robin read of enchantments and spells. At dawn the sorcerer awoke and found the apprentice laying the table for breakfast, unaware that the lad had begun his apprenticeship in earnest.

Night after night the apprentice returned to the sorcerer's room to study. He learned many wonders—potions, charms, and words of transformation. Occasionally he tested his newfound knowledge with simple experiments: changing a pebble into a peacock; ash into gold; or a bumblebee into a bear then back again.

At times he was successful. But when he was not, the words became confused and swarmed in his tired brain. Then, feeling too small and weak to stop his master's evil plan, he would rest his weary head in his hands and weep.

One evening the sorcerer descended the stairs and triumphantly announced that all was ready.

"Tomorrow," he gloated, "I will unleash my masterpiece of vengeance. The sky will become as black as a raven's wing, and out of the blackness will come their doom."

The apprentice was too frightened to ask what form the doom would take. He quickly laid the table for the man's supper and, after the meal, when the sorcerer was asleep, the lad crept to the golden cage.

"Little dove, it is too late," he moaned. "I have failed."

"It is not too late," she cried, "there is still one night left. Go, you may yet discover what the sorcerer is plotting and find a way to alter his wicked plan."

As the apprentice entered his master's chamber, a chill of dread seized him. By the candlelight, he could see the black, iron-bound volume lying open on the table. The sorcerer, in his excitement, had forgotten to lock it.

Word by word, Robin read the spidery script and gasped with horror. Out of the blackness would come a terror to spoil every man, woman, and child's sleep forever — nightmares!

"How can I stop that?" he gasped. Then he remembered the dove's words. "You may yet discover what the sorcerer is plotting and find a way to alter his wicked plan."

He could do it! He sharpened the end of a twig and blackened its tip in the candle's flame. Using it as a pen, the lad skillfully altered the wording of the spell, praying that the sorcerer would not discover the deceit until it was too late.

Next morning Robin waited anxiously as the sorcerer added the final ingredients to the potion.

Toadstool, adder's tongue, dragon's horn, lizard's lung.
Mandrake root, devil's paw, hembane, nightshade, goblin's claw.
Ear of bat, skin of newt, boil and stir with hemp and jute.

Holding the book of evil open to the page, the sorcerer began to pronounce the words of the spell. Thunder shook the room and the cauldron began to rock crazily on the burning coals.

A flash of lightning sprang from its centre and the maker of all nightmares suddenly rose before them, howling wildly, its terrible eyes glowing like flame.

At the sorcerer's command, the monster stopped its shrill roar and began to swallow air. With every breath it grew, until it towered above them.

The sorcerer pranced and jumped with joy, while the creature, swollen like a hideous balloon, glared down upon them.

"Fly," cackled the sorcerer, "fly." The monster took a deep breath, raised itself as if to obey, and suddenly exploded. In its place, tiny golden bubbles drifted gently on the air.

Stunned, the sorcerer grasped the book and traced every line of the verse to find where he had erred. As he did, the words of the spell smudged, and examining his finger, he found it had become stained with charcoal.

Someone had tampered with his book, someone who could read and write. The mystery took only a moment to solve. The apprentice had outwitted him. With a terrible fury, the man rushed at the lad.

Robin dashed for the door.

"Stop," cried the sorcerer, "you shall not escape," and he grabbed for the lad's collar.

The apprentice, speaking a powerful incantation, changed into a mighty stag and disappeared into the wood.

The sorcerer, mad with fury, sprang after him and, as he did, became a ferocious wolf.

Although the stag was swift, the forest was so dense and twisted that he soon became trapped. The wolf found him and, with lips curled back to reveal teeth like daggers, circled for the kill. As he leapt, the apprentice uttered a magic phrase and changed into a swallow that soared high above the trees. His master was equal to this and, with a single word, changed from a wolf to a hawk.

Try as he might, the lad could not compete with the sorcerer's tremendous speed. Diving down upon him, the hawk sank its razor-sharp talons deep into the swallow's outstretched wings. The apprentice gasped with pain, certain his end had come. Suddenly the lad had a master stroke and, quick as a flash, became a boulder. Down through the clouds they fell, the hawk struggling desperately in the grip of the stone. With a mighty spell, the sorcerer broke free, but it was too late. Crashing down, his life came to an end and, with it, his evil ways.

The apprentice was unharmed and ran back to the house with the joyful news that the sorcerer was dead.

He opened the golden cage to free the dove. The bird flew from its prison and glided around the room.

As it did, a miraculous change took place. Instead of the dove, a beautiful maiden with shining eyes and flowing black hair stood before him.

"Your courage has freed me from the sorcerer's spell and saved my people," she said. It was the Princess, now grown into a young woman. She told Robin how the sorcerer had transformed her into a dove and stolen her away.

"For your bravery and kindness, you deserve a reward. Ask whatever your heart desires," she said, "and if it is in my power to give, you shall receive it."

There was only one thing Robin desired and that was the maiden's hand in marriage.

"It is as I hoped," she said sweetly, hearing the apprentice's request, "for that is also the wish of my heart."

Together they travelled back to the maiden's land. The people rejoiced to have their beloved Princess return to them.

A great wedding banquet was held and, after the ceremony, they were crowned King and Queen. Their reign was long and happy and the kingdom prospered as it never had before, for together they used their powers for the good and benefit of all.